Jean Van Leeuwen • pictures by Henri Sorensen

# A Fourth of July on the Plains

Dial Books for Young Readers  New York

Published by Dial Books for Young Readers | A Division of Penguin Books USA Inc.
375 Hudson Street | New York, New York 10014

3 5 7 9 10 8 6 4 2

Library of Congress Cataloging in Publication Data
Van Leeuwen, Jean.
A Fourth of July on the plains | by Jean Van Leeuwen; pictures by Henri Sorensen.
p.   cm.
Summary: Young Jesse and his family are with a wagon train traveling from Indiana
to Oregon when they stop to celebrate the Fourth of July, but Jesse is too young to go
hunting with the men, so he comes up with his own contribution to the festivities.
ISBN 0-8037-1771-7.—ISBN 0-8037-1772-5 (lib. bdg.)
[1. Frontier and pioneer life—Fiction.   2. Overland journeys to the Pacific—
Fiction.   3. Fourth of July—Fiction.]   I. Sorensen, Henri, ill.   II. Title.
PZ7.V3273Fo   1997   [E]—dc20   94-33172   CIP   AC

*The artwork was rendered in watercolor, ink pen, and colored pencils.*

"...the young men marched round the camp
this evening after supper, whistling Yank Doodle..."

*Eugenia Zieber, July 4, 1851*

---

This story is based on an account of a July 4th celebration along
the Oregon Trail in 1852, as recalled in the Diary of E. W. Conyers
(Transactions of the Oregon Pioneer Association, 1905). I am also
indebted to many other travelers' writings about the trail, and es-
pecially to the lively memories of Jesse A. Applegate, a seven-
year-old traveler, as told in *Recollections of My Boyhood* (Review
Publishing Co., 1914).     *J.V.L.*

To Evelyne and Bud Johnson
*H.S.*

We'd been traveling so long, I could barely remember what it felt like to sleep in a real bed in our log cabin back home in Indiana.

Eight weeks, Ma said. And still we were not even halfway to Oregon.

In those eight weeks, I'd worn out my shoes so I had to go barefoot, picking prickly-pear thorns out of my toes.

I'd lost my hat crossing a river and seen three cattle drown.

I'd slept outside in hailstorms.

I'd looked into the proud painted faces of Indians, and chased after buffalo.

I'd fallen out of the wagon trying to crack Pa's whip and near been run over by the wheels. Pa said it was a miracle I was still alive.

Now we were camped in a little valley near a river called the Sweetwater, where the grass was knee-deep. Here we would stay, Pa said, resting the weary cattle till after the Fourth of July.

The Fourth of July! At home it was a day of booming cannons and flying flags, parades and speechifying and games. How could we celebrate way out here on the plains?

That was the talk I heard around the campfires that night.

"A picnic," suggested one of the ladies. And everyone agreed. "Not just a picnic, but a feast for the glorious Fourth!"

So early next morning, preparations began. Some of the men went hunting for game up in the mountains. My biggest brother, Henry, saddled up our horse to go with them. I scrambled on behind.

"Not you, Jesse," said Pa, plucking me off.

I had to watch as they disappeared into the dusty hills.

The older boys went off to gather wood for the fires. I tagged along behind my next biggest brothers, Luther and Ben.

"Not you, Jesse!" called Ma.

I kept walking, pretending not to hear. But next thing I knew, her firm fingers had me by the shirt collar.

"Aw, Ma!" I protested.

"I want to keep an eye on you, you rascal!" she said.

She'd been keeping a sharp eye on me since the day I climbed into the wrong wagon and fell asleep and for five hours she thought I was lost.

In camp there was nothing to do but pick up sticks with my little brother Sam and my cousin Willy. We watched men taking wagons apart to make long tables for the feast. And women beginning their baking. And some older girls trying to sew a flag.

One had an old sheet and another a torn red skirt.

"These will make the stripes," they said. "But where will we get the field of blue?"

My big sisters, Amelia and Lucy, went from wagon to wagon, but all they could find was a lavender sunbonnet. Then Lucy whispered something to Ma. She nodded. Lucy ran to our wagon and came back with a faded blue jacket of Pa's. "Will this do?" she asked.

Smiling, the girls took out needles and thread and began to sew.

My legs were itching to be doing something.

"Race you to the wagon!" I cried to Sam and Willy.

We dropped our sticks and ran.

I was the fastest, sure to win. But suddenly I tripped over a tent peg. I went sprawling, right on top of a pan of Ma's bread dough rising in the grass.

"Jesse, you scamp!"

Now I was in for it. Ma had me by the ear this time. She sat me down next to her by the cooking fire and handed me a wooden spoon.

"Stir this pot," she ordered. "And don't you dare move."

All afternoon I sat there. The girls finished their flag. The hunters returned, carrying an antelope, several sage hens, four fat jackrabbits, and a surprise: a giant snowball.

I couldn't believe my eyes. "A snowball in July?"

"Way up in those mountains," said Henry, "the snow never melts."

Luther and Ben dragged in a dead tree close to twenty feet tall.

"Here is our flagpole," they told Pa.

"Good job, boys!" he said.

Everything was ready for the big celebration. And everyone but me had helped. I scowled into Ma's cooking fire. What could I do for the glorious Fourth?

I thought of last year when Pa had taken us to town. We had listened to long speeches that near put me to sleep. We'd watched footraces and shooting matches and a parade, with soldiers marching and fifes and drums tooting and tapping.

Music! That was what we needed. Suddenly I had the most glorious idea.

"Sam! Willy!" I whispered my idea in their ears. And the three of us began to grin.

The sky was still dark next morning when explosions filled the air.

Heads peered fearfully out of tents and wagons.

"What was that?" Ma asked sleepily.

A dozen men were firing rifles in the air.

"We cannot greet the day with cannons," one said, laughing. "So this will have to do."

As the sun rose, coloring the sky pink, the men slowly raised the flagpole with our flag nailed to the top.  To me it looked mighty fine, fluttering in the breeze. Everyone gathered round and sang "The Star-spangled Banner." Then it was time for the speeches.

A man from Missouri stood up on a table and read the Declaration of Independence. After that came the oration, by Dr. Harvey Witherspoon of Illinois. I knew it would go on a long time. For once Ma's eyes were on the speaker, not me. This was our chance.

"Now!" I whispered to Sam and Willy, and we slipped away.

In Willy's tent, George and Andy and Tom and Virgil were waiting.

"Have you got everything?" I asked.

They had tin dishes and wooden spoons. A cowbell that had mysteriously disappeared from around the neck of Andy's family's milk cow. A whistle borrowed from Virgil's brother Homer. And our big washtub that I'd pinched from our wagon while Ma's back was turned.

"Perfect," I said.

We waited. And waited. It looked like Dr. Witherspoon was fixing to go on speechifying till sundown.

Tom tapped on his tin pan. Virgil blew a few soft notes, practicing.

"Sssh!" I whispered. "It's got to be a surprise."

At last we heard clapping and cheering.

"It's our turn now," I told them.

Out of the tent we marched, whistling "Yankee Doodle." Virgil tweeted on his whistle. Andy rang his cowbell. And I beat loudly on my new bass drum.

*Rat-a-tat! Tweet-tweet!* It was just like a parade with fifes and drums.

Around tents and wagons and campfires we marched. Around tables, then up to the flagpole. Little children fell in behind us. Men were whistling and ladies clapping. I saw Ma's face, and it was smiling.

Soon everyone joined in the singing.

"Father and I went down to camp
Along with Captain Goodwin,
And there we saw the men and boys
As thick as hasty puddin'.
Yankee Doodle, keep it up,
Yankee Doodle dandy.
Mind the music and the step
And with the girls be handy."

We marched and drummed and whistled and sang. My drum was just
as loud as the soldiers', I thought happily. Then I happened to see the sky.
It had turned black. That wasn't my drum I was hearing, but thunder!
"Storm's coming!" someone shouted. "Take down the flag!"
Everyone raced for the wagons and tents as rain poured out of the sky.

I ducked under a wagon with Sam and Willy. Lightning flashed. Thunder boomed, like cannons firing. Sam covered his ears, but I was laughing. We had our cannons after all.

Then, as fast as it had come up, the storm was over. Rain dripped. The sun came out. And I heard one of the young men cry, "Bring on the feast!"
Moments later the tables were piled high. I hadn't seen so much food since last Christmas dinner at Grandma's house.

There was roast antelope, sage hen stew, and jackrabbit potpie. Irish potatoes brought all the way from Ohio, baked beans and rice, pickles and preserves. Bread and biscuits hot from the oven. Coffee, tea, and cold mountain stream water to drink. And for dessert, pound cake and jelly cake and peach, dried apple, and strawberry pies. And best of all, bowls piled high with Sweetwater mountain ice cream, made from our giant snowball.

I ate till I thought I would burst.

When at last the eating was done, a young man leaped up on the table.

"Three cheers for our flag, Old Glory!" he cried.

"Hip, hip, hooray!" everyone shouted.

"And three cheers for the ladies who gave us this feast!"

"Hip, hip, hooray!"

"And three more for our band of young music-makers!"

"Hip, hip, hooray!"

I jumped up next to him and took a deep bow.

It was a glorious Fourth of July, one I would never forget.

Next year, though, out in Oregon, I aimed to march in a real parade, beating on a real bass drum. Maybe I would enter the shooting matches. And the footrace too.

I could win the footrace. I knew I could.